BAX and his BUBBLES

All About A Kid and His Thoughts

This book belongs to:

_____

Dr. Sonia E. Amin

Illustrated by Pardeep Mehra

To my precious boys,
Asaiah and Malachi.
You are my inspiration.

soniaeamin.com

Published in the United States by Sanasamal Press.

Library of Congress Control Number: 2020941409

Illustrations by Pardeep Mehra
Edited by Bobbie Hinman
Cover & Layout by Praise Saflor
Project Managed by April Cox

Publisher's Cataloging-in-Publication Data

Names: Amin, Sonia E., author. | Mehra, Pardeep, illustrator.
Title: Bax and his bubbles : all about a kid and his thoughts / Dr. Sonia E. Amin; Pardeep Mehra.
Description: Debary, FL: Sanasamal Press, 2020. | Summary: A young boy learns to think positive thoughts and let go of negative ones.
Identifiers: LCCN: 2020941409 | ISBN: 978-1-7352996-2-4 (Hardcover) | 978-1-7352996-0-0 (pbk.) | 978-1-7352996-1-7 (ebook)
Subjects: LCSH Positive psychology--Juvenile literature. | Mindfulness (Psychology)--Juvenile literature. | Attitude (Psychology)--Juvenile literature. | CYAC Positive psychology. | Mindfulness (Psychology). | Attitude (Psychology) | BISAC JUVENILE FICTION / Social Themes / Emotions & Feelings
Classification: LCC BF698.35.057 A45 2020 | DDC 155.4/191--dc23

A Note to Grown-ups

One of the most important gifts you can give the children in your life is helping them understand the power of their thoughts. Recognizing the role their thoughts play in what they choose to say and do is their first step toward intentionally focusing their minds on thoughts they allow.

The inspiration for the mental fortitude discussed in this book is the biblical scripture Philippians 4:8 (NLT):

> Fix your thoughts on what is true, and honorable, and right, and pure, and lovely and admirable. Think about things that are excellent and worthy of praise.

The appealing visual of a beautiful bubble illuminates this scriptural concept to children.

At the end of this book are discussion starters for asking children about their thoughts after reading this story. Discussions like these encourage children to stop and think when they are having a hard time with their thoughts. Additionally, reassuring them that they can talk to you when they are struggling is a wonderful way to establish open communication.

Whether you are a parent, teacher, or counselor, I hope this book becomes a useful tool for the children in your life. I am praying for you and the children you care for, as *Bax and His Bubbles* helps them take a simple step toward being purposeful in their thought life.

Thoughtfully Yours,

Sonia Amin

This is **Bax.**

Bax has lots of bubbles.

I am kind.

Today is going to be a good day.

I am creative.

It's okay to make mistakes.

I am a hard worker.

Playing soccer is so much fun!

These are thought bubbles. Inside each bubble is something Bax is thinking. Everything Bax says or does starts with a thought inside his head.

Sometimes Bax has happy thoughts.

I love playing with my brother.

My parents love me.

Some of his thoughts are filled with surprise and excitement.

But with so many thoughts, how does Bax know which bubbles to keep and which ones to let go?

Bax takes time to THINK.

He also talks to his Mom and Dad.

"How do I know which bubbles to keep?" he asks.

Mom answers, "Keep the bubbles that are filled with good thoughts. Then let go of the bubbles filled with mean or hurtful thoughts."

Dad adds, "Release those mean bubbles and let them float away. Hold onto the bubbles that are filled with TRUE... and KIND...and EXCELLENT thoughts."

"Yes, I can do that!" says Bax.

Bax THINKS about his BUBBLES.
If he has a thought that is not TRUE, then he can release it from his mind and let that bubble go.

I'm not good at anything.

"Hmm, that's really not true," he thinks.
"I will let this bubble go."

Mom suggests thinking TRUE thoughts about things he can do to become better at soccer. Bax replaces the UNTRUE thought with a TRUE thought.

Bax thinks...

There are also times that Bax has thought bubbles that are not KIND. The UNKIND bubbles are filled with thoughts that may be mean or hurtful to others.

"That's not a very kind thought, Bax," says Mom. "If you say that to your brother, you will hurt his feelings. Think about all the fun you have with him and how great it is to have a brother. Is this a bubble you want to let go?"

"Bye-bye, UNKIND bubble," says Bax as he lets go and watches it float away, taking the UNKIND feelings along with it.

"I'm proud of you for letting that bubble go," says his mom.

Most of the time, Bax has bubbles filled with EXCELLENT thoughts. These are the ones he keeps. Bax may even choose to SPEAK or ACT ON his EXCELLENT thoughts...

like the day he saw a new student in the cafeteria sitting all by herself.

There was even a time that he wanted to raise money to buy toys for sick children at the local hospital.

And so he did.
"Get your lemonade! Just 50¢ a cup!"

Bax knows that with every thought he has,
he also has a choice of what to do with that thought.

He can hold onto bubbles filled with TRUE thoughts. He can
release bubbles filled with thoughts that are UNTRUE and
UNKIND. He can let them go...up...up...and away...

He can also choose to replace those bubbles with ones that
have EXCELLENT thoughts.

His mom explains: "Although some thoughts are not so nice, it's normal to have negative thoughts sometimes. Everyone has them. It's important to recognize those thoughts. We then have a choice of what we do with them. Always remember, we have the power to choose which thoughts we keep."

When Bax chooses to let his negative thoughts go, he replaces them with positive thoughts. Bax doesn't always get it right, but he tries his best.

Negative thoughts

"Bye-bye, negative thoughts," he says.

Bax takes time to THINK and chooses to think THOUGHTS that are TRUE, KIND and EXCELLENT.

Is this thought TRUE?

Is this thought KIND?

Is this thought EXCELLENT?

Let's Talk About It

The questions listed here will help you foster discussions with your child. Please feel free to adapt the questions to suit your child's age and maturity level.

Pre-Reading Discussion Questions:

1. What clue does the title give you about the book?
2. What does the cover illustration make you think of?
3. Do you have any questions before reading the book?

During-Reading Discussion Questions:

1. Who is the main character?
2. How would you describe him?
3. How do facial expressions help you guess how someone might be feeling?
4. How are you and Bax alike?
5. What does this book remind you of?

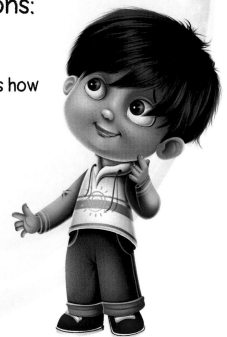

After-Reading Discussion Questions:

1. What was your favorite part of the story?
2. How do you think your THOUGHTS can affect the things you choose to say and do?
3. Although Bax was upset when he did not get the soccer ball in the goal, he chose to let go of his UNTRUE thought and replace it with a TRUE thought. When was there a time you were upset and thought something that was not true, and chose to let that thought bubble go?
4. Who are the grownups in your life that you trust and can talk to about your thought bubbles?

After-Reading Activity:

Go outside with a grownup and enjoy blowing bubbles! Think of all the TRUE, KIND, and EXCELLENT thoughts all those bubbles could be. Have fun!

Thank You!

Sign up to hear about free downloads and more!
You can also schedule an author school visit or
sponsor your school with copies of the book.

Visit soniaeamin.com for more information.

If you enjoyed Bax and His Bubbles, we would love
to hear from you! Reviews are incredibly valuable
to authors. Please consider leaving a review on
Amazon and sharing a picture on social media.
#baxandhisbubbles

About the
Author

Sonia Amin is a wife, mother, and pharmacist who loves encouraging others with her words, hugs, and prayers. She lives in Florida with her husband and two kids and considers herself to be a professional *snuggler* to each of them. Inspired by the books she enjoys reading with her kids, she has fulfilled her dream of writing one herself. She invites you to reach out to her online at soniaeamin.com.

About the
Illustrator

Pardeep Mehra, is the founder of Pencil Master Digital Studio, a family-owned business providing end to end illustration and publishing services. For more than 15 years, Pardeep has been providing his keen eye, visualization and digital art skills to create books that delight children all over the world. Pardeep lives in India with his wife and daughter. For more info visit www.pencilmasterdigi.com.

Acknowledgements

To my husband — Thank you for holding my hand, loving me, and encouraging me to work for the dream I've had for so long. This book would not have been possible without you and all your support, day in and day out. You are my rock.

To my parents — Thank you for all your love, prayers, and support through everything in life, including this journey. Your dedication to God and the sacrifices you made are what brought me to where I am today. I am forever grateful.

To my sister — Thank you for believing in me even when I didn't. Thank you for your endless words of encouragement and for speaking words of life every time I needed it. I cannot put into words the blessing you are to me.

To my family, friends and everyone on my team — Thank you for being my cheerleaders and supporting me through this entire endeavor. Without you all, this book would not be what it is.